The Life and Canine Times of Pee Wee and Buddy

PAGE PUBLISHING, INC.
Conneaut Lake, PA

First originally published by Page Publishing 2021

ISBN 978-1-6624-3411-2 (pbk)
ISBN 978-1-6624-3412-9 (digital)

Printed in the United States of America

The Life and Canine Times of
Pee Wee
and
Buddy

Casey Gent and Todd Gent

Preface

Pee Wee and Buddy, a dachshund/corgi mix and three-legged beagle/basset, respectively, are based on actual family pets of the author, Casey, and her brother, Coby. Todd, their father, co-wrote The Life and Canine Times of Pee Wee and Buddy, in which he and his daughter hope to teach readers how to treat others with loving-kindness and good ole-fashioned manners.

Pee Wee's best friend in the book is based on Coby, Todd's son and Casey's brother, who suffered from cystic fibrosis (CF) and passed in 2008. Coby persevered through many hospital stays and surgeries, including a double-lung transplant when he was just thirteen years old.

The Gents are a tight-knit family who came together to keep Coby alive and as healthy as someone with CF could be.

The two rescue dogs in the story lived to be eighteen years old and were great companions and friends to the family. Todd and Casey use the dogs and their everyday lives to teach kids and adults alike to befriend everyone and stick together when others are not so kind.

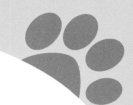

His name was Pee Wee.

Pee Wee was black with brown touches. It looked like he stepped in brown paint with those big paws when he was born. It was as if he were wiping sweat off his brow and the brown paint just stuck above his eyes, making permanent eyebrows.

Pee Wee was a part dachshund and part corgi.

He was what his new best friend and the other pups called a lowrider.

Pee Wee started in Orlando, Florida, and ended up in the rescue because his last owner became ill and had to go into a nursing home.

The folks at the rescue took Pee Wee's picture and had him write an e-mail to tell all about himself and how he liked to play with his big red ball.

It seemed Pee Wee was destined for Destin, Florida, because his new best friend was a Texas transplant who lived there. He had seen Pee Wee's picture and read his e-mail.

He wanted Pee Wee right away.

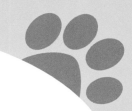

So Pee Wee packed up his red ball, the one in his younger days he liked to chase. Nowadays, in his older years, he was looking for something to take its place.

Pee Wee hitched a ride from Orlando to Destin. He was happier than a hound dog in a pickup truck! He was then introduced to his new best friend, who did not seem to feel well all the time. Some days, he just had to stay in the bed.

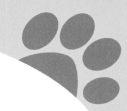

Pee Wee would stay by his side with his new best friend always petting him on his head and giving him belly rubs.

No matter how Pee Wee's best friend felt, he always treated Pee Wee like a king, spoiling him with treats and even food off his own plate.

Pee Wee learned he liked the "ham out," also known as the handout.

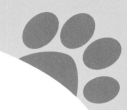

Pee Wee's best friend had a sister with a dog named Buddy.

Buddy had one blue eye and one brown eye. Not only that, but Buddy only had three legs because he had been hit by a car.

"Yeah, got caught with my nose on a scent," Buddy had told Pee Wee. "It was a hit-and-run," Buddy said.

Buddy did not seem too down about losing his leg. "I've got three others that work just fine," he was known to say.

Buddy was also a rescue dog and was the same age as Pee Wee.

Buddy was a part beagle and part basset hound. He sure could howl, even when the moon was not out.

Pee Wee took it upon himself to walk the perimeter of his new big backyard.

He liked when the grass was freshly mowed so it did not rub and tickle his belly.

He and Buddy liked to patrol the backyard so they could keep out undesirables, such as snakes and mice, that could bring harm to their best friends.

Pee Wee would alert his best friend with a bark, and Buddy with a deep, loud howl.

Squirrels used the electric company's high-power line as a shortcut. They stopped along the way to taunt the dogs with their tails, shaking and speaking their squirrel chatter.

All Pee Wee and Buddy could do was look up and bark and hope that one day that squirrel would have a misstep and fall into the yard. Then the dogs would have a squirrel by the tail!

Until that day, they would just look up and bark away without realizing they were getting exercise that would help them be able to play.

An occasional plane or helicopter would fly by because the airport was nearby. This also got the dogs a-barking and a-running!

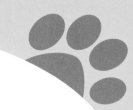

The two also liked the backyard because they could roam and prowl without a leash.

"I prefer the harness to that choker thing!" Buddy once said.

"Yep, me too," Pee Wee agreed. "Too bad it's the leash law, or I wouldn't be wearing anything at all!"

Pee Wee and Buddy took daily walks together and were accompanied by the sister of Pee Wee's best friend. The two dogs had much to say about what they saw and smelled in their Florida neighborhood.

They always dodged the water sprinklers, or water stinklers, as Buddy referred to them.

"What's with all the trash?" Pee Wee asked, dodging a paper plate. "They don't think of us four-leggers, oh, I mean sometimes three-leggers. Sorry, Buddy. Some of this stuff is sharp and could cut our paws."

"Yep, the trash could even hurt our best friends too."

There were all kinds of dogs walking with their best friends.

The snotty poodle was out, along with her snotty owner.

"What's that thing she always does with her eyes?" Pee Wee asked about the poodle's best friend.

"Oh, the eye roll?" Buddy answered. "She thinks she is a bit better than the rest of us."

"Well, she ought to look where she's going sometimes so she won't step on the trash!" Pee Wee chimed in.

"Why are those dogs so tall and lean?" Pee Wee asked. "Man, those are retired racing dogs, greyhounds," Buddy answered. "They're built for speed!"

"I'm built more like a speed bump," Pee Wee added.

"Yeah, but that way you can see the small print in the newspaper better because you are closer," Buddy joked. "If you read the paper, that is," he added.

"You smell that?" Buddy and Pee Wee both stuck their noses in the air.

"Somebody's grilling some fish," Buddy noted. "Wouldn't mind getting a sample of that!" Pee Wee said, and Buddy agreed.

Other dogs in the neighborhood barked from their windows or backyards as Buddy and Pee Wee explored. "Hey, Shorty! Hey, Tripod!" the bully dogs would make fun of Pee Wee being low to the ground and Buddy missing a leg.

The two senior dogs did not pay the bullies any mind and just kept on cruising along down the street. After all, they had each other and their best friends who loved them no matter what.

"What's it matter what some bully says anyway?" Buddy told Pee Wee.

"Yeah, what pedigree do they think they are?" Pee Wee added. "I know dogs I met in the shelter who were mixed with three or four breeds, and they weren't bullies. They were fun to bark with."

Sometimes Pee Wee did not have to walk because his best friend took him for a ride in his car. Pee Wee loved sticking his head out of the window and letting his ears catch the wind.

From the passenger window, he watched the world go by fast.

Buddy liked riding in his best friend's little red truck. He, too, enjoyed the breeze flowing through his brown-and-white fur as he stuck his nose out of the passenger window.

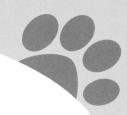

Buddy and Pee Wee loved going to the dog park and nosing around with the other dogs.

There were a few exceptions, though. The yapping Chihuahua got on their nerves, but they accepted every dog and just went along, minding their own business.

Buddy received many stares from other dog owners because he was missing a leg. "I would expect this from that big bully dog, but not his best friends," Buddy would say.

"Anyways, I've got three other legs that work just fine."

"You know, Pee Wee, if us senior dogs stick together, we could be some real game changers," Buddy said.

Pee Wee just agreed, and the two loaded up in the car.

On occasion, Pee Wee and Buddy's best friends left the house. Pee Wee and Buddy were left alone to patrol the inside of the place. The senior dogs would have a good conversation about years past and bark at passersby, including the garbage men. Pee Wee looked out to hear the arm of the garbage truck grabbing the trash can. Buddy said, "You can bark, but they are going to take the garbage whether you do or not."

Sometimes the fellows would just nap until their best friends returned. When that would be, they never knew but waited anxiously for them to come back.

The dogs sure would get to barking when the man would mow the back alley. They would run out the dog door that led to the yard and bark and howl as the mower zoomed by.

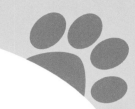

The electric garage door finally made a sound, announcing the arrival of Pee Wee and Buddy's best friends, who had been gone for what seemed to the dogs was forever. It may only have been fifteen minutes, but in a dog's life, that was quite a long time.

"I never thought they were coming home," Pee Wee told Buddy.

"Same here!" Buddy replied and then howled to greet his best friend and her brother.

About the Author

Casey Gent graduated from high school in Wylie, Texas, in 1999. She attended the Universidad de Colima and lived with a family in Mexico during her first year of college. From there, she moved to Destin, Florida, and graduated from the University of West Florida in Pensacola. Casey's hope for *The Life and Canine Times of Pee Wee and Buddy* is to teach kids and adults the importance of accepting people as they are and living a life of loving-kindness. Seeing the world through the eyes of Pee Wee, Buddy, and those they cross paths with will hopefully influence young minds to be kinder, more empathetic, and less judgmental.

Todd Gent, the father of Casey, is a retired coach, teacher, and X-ray technician. He resides in Oak Grove, Texas, with his wife, Tricia. By using animals and dog humor in *The Life and Canine Times of Pee Wee and Buddy*, Todd and his daughter, Casey, have collaborated to teach kids as well as adults about kindness, acceptance, and living every day to the fullest. Inspired by real pets of the family who showed nothing but unconditional love, Todd and Casey hope to use these animals' positive way of living to influence readers, young and old.

CPSIA information can be obtained
at www.ICGtesting.com
Printed in the USA
BVHW061044020821
613410BV00004B/37